DISNEY
PRINCESS

My Princess Collection

Jasmine

Soaring to the Skies

Book Eight

Chapter One

My name is Princess Jasmine. My father is the Sultan of Agrabah. I'm married to my true love, Aladdin.

Before I met Aladdin, I didn't want to be a princess. All Father thought about was finding a husband for me. The law said I had to marry before my next birthday.

I thought it was a stupid law. I didn't want to marry because I had to. I wanted to marry for love!

Then there was Jafar, the royal vizier. He had been my father's adviser for years, but I didn't trust him. My pet tiger, Rajah, and I watched him and his parrot, Iago. They were planning something. I just knew it!

I realized Father only wanted the best for me, but I couldn't marry someone I didn't even know. I decided to leave the palace and see the world.

I disguised myself as a peasant, and with Rajah's help, I climbed over the garden wall to the streets of Agrabah. I was free!

Chapter Two

The city was amazing. While exploring a busy market, I gave an apple to a hungry boy. The street vendor asked me how I planned to pay for it. When I told him I didn't have any money, he grabbed my arm!

Suddenly, a stranger appeared. "Thank you, kind sir," he said to the vendor. He explained that I was his crazy sister.

The street vendor didn't believe us and called for the palace guards! We ran away, and the stranger led me to his rooftop hideout.

The stranger's name was Aladdin. He asked me where I was from.

"What does it matter?" I asked. I wanted to be just like Aladdin—free to do what I wanted and to live by my own rules.

We sat and looked at the view. "The palace looks pretty amazing," Aladdin said.

Aladdin told me he dreamed about living there. I wanted to tell him that life on the streets was so much better than living inside the palace. But I didn't want him to know who I really was.

Time passed quickly as we talked about our dreams. Aladdin was

honest and real. He didn't pretend to be
anything that he wasn't.

Suddenly, the royal guards appeared. "Here
you are!" they shouted, waving their swords.

Aladdin looked me in the eyes and held
out his hand. "Do you trust me?" he asked. I
did, so I took his hand in mine and we
jumped.

We landed safely and started running through the alleyways, but the guards caught up to us. I pulled off my scarf to show them who I was. "Release him!" I ordered.

"Sorry, Princess," the captain said. "We have orders from Jafar."

Aladdin was quite surprised to discover that I was the Sultan's daughter and not a peasant.

When I returned to the palace, I asked Jafar where Aladdin was. He told me Aladdin had been sentenced to death for kidnapping me.

"He didn't kidnap me!" I protested.

"Oh, dear!" Jafar replied. "The sentence has already been carried out."

I ran out of the room, collapsed by a fountain, and wept.

Chapter Three

The next day, hundreds of people filled the streets of Agrabah. A loud parade marched toward the palace with dancers, music—and even an elephant.

The parade was in honor of a prince named Ali Ababwa. I was still heartbroken over Aladdin, and I didn't want to meet some arrogant prince. But if he really wanted to see me, I'd tell him exactly how I felt!

After Father welcomed the prince, he called for me. I marched into the throne room.

Father really liked him, but this prince was even worse than the others, strutting around in fancy clothes like a peacock.

"How dare you decide my future?" I asked Prince Ali, angrily. "I'm not a prize to be won!" Then I stormed out of the room.

Chapter Four

I was in my room when Rajah ran out to the balcony. He growled at Prince Ali, who had suddenly appeared on the balcony.

"I don't want to see you," I told him. "Go jump off a balcony!"

Ali apologized and did just that.

"No!" I cried in fear.

But Ali didn't fall. Instead he seemed to be floating in midair.

"How are you doing that?" I asked.

"It's a Magic Carpet—do you want to go for a ride?" Ali asked. He reached out his hand. "Do you trust me?"

I had heard those words once before, spoken by Aladdin. Could they be the same person? I needed to know. "Yes," I said, taking his hand.

That night, we explored faraway places that I had only read about. And he revealed that he really *was* Aladdin. I was so happy that he was alive!

When we got back to my balcony, Aladdin gave me a kiss. We had fallen in love with each other. And I made up my mind— Aladdin was the man I was going to marry.

Chapter Five

The next morning, I went to tell Father my news. He was standing with Jafar.

"You will wed Jafar," he said strangely. Father looked as if he had been hypnotized!

Just then, Aladdin burst into the room. He told us that Jafar had tried to kill him the night before.

What did Jafar want with Aladdin? I soon found out.

Aladdin had discovered a magic lamp and become friends with the Genie who lived inside it. The Genie transformed Aladdin into Prince Ali in order to impress me. But Jafar had stolen Aladdin's lamp, and now all of the Genie's powers were in Jafar's evil hands.

Jafar had always wanted to be sultan—with me as his queen. Now that he had hypnotized my father and taken over Agrabah, Jafar commanded the Genie to make me love him. He didn't know that genies can't make people fall in love. So, I just pretended to be in love with Jafar.

While Jafar looked into my eyes, Aladdin searched for the lamp. But Jafar saw through the trick and trapped me in an hourglass.

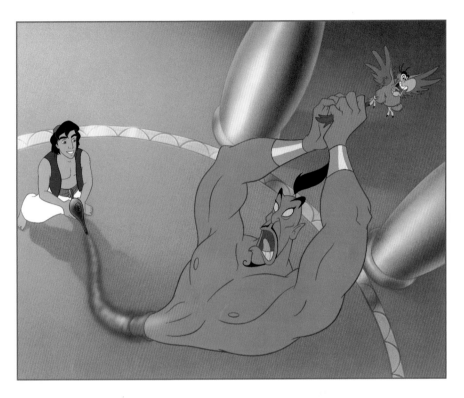

Then Aladdin had an idea. He fooled Jafar
into making one last wish: to be the most
powerful genie in the world. Jafar turned into
a genie, but he had forgotten something. A
genie has to live inside a magic lamp until
someone frees him. Jafar was now trapped!

Father thanked Aladdin and the Genie for saving Agrabah. He then changed the law. The Princess of Agrabah could now choose to marry whomever she wanted . . . whenever she wanted. I chose Aladdin, of course.

Then Aladdin and I set off on the Magic Carpet to explore a whole new world . . . together.